ANDRO, Star of Bethlehem

written by Anne Cl
illustrated by Nan P

Published by The STANDARD PUBLISHING Company, Cincinnati, Ohio
Division of STANDEX INTERNATIONAL Corporation. Printed in U.S.A.

Andro Star slid into his place on the front row. He was covered with bright flashes of cosmic dust. And he was late to the star choir practice. Again!

"I'm sorry. I'm sorry. I am very sorry, sir, for being late," Andro stammered as the Great Singing Star looked down at him from the choir director's box. "I was—well, it was like this, sir. I was watching a gigantic meteoroid zapping and zooming all over the sky. Oh, sir, it was the fastest 'n the biggest one I've ever seen! And, well, I guess I forgot it was time for choir practice!"

Great Singing Star glowed with impatient flashes of red and orange. "Excuses! Excuses!" he muttered, tapping his baton for silence.

Immediately the stars became quiet. Each one was watching, waiting, ready to sing. At the director's signal, they burst into song.

Andro Star sang in his loudest voice, and with all his heart.

Suddenly, Great Singing Star lowered his arms and rapped his baton. All singing stopped.

"Someone is not singing in tune!" he announced. His eyes moved slowly along the front row. "Let me hear you sing your part," he said, pointing his baton at Andro.

"ME?" Andro squeaked. "You mean *me*? Me? Sing all by myself?"

"Yes, you!" Great Singing Star nodded.

Andro took a deep breath. He cleared his throat. He took another deep breath. Then he opened his mouth wide and sang his very best.

The other choir stars looked at one another. Some even laughed.

"Andro Star," Great Singing Star said sadly, "You are not singing your part in tune. And you must be in tune if you sing with the star choir before the Lord God. Go, practice your part. You'll have one more time to try at the next choir practice."

"Oh thank you, sir, *thank you!!*" Andro said as he jetted off to a far corner in the heavens.

And there he practiced and practiced all night long. More than anything else in the universe, Andro wanted to sing praises to the Lord God with the star choir.

At the next choir practice, Andro slid into his place early. And when the singing started, he sang his best. But this time, *softly*. He hoped Great Singing Star would not hear him, just in case he was not singing in tune.

But Great Singing Star *did* hear. He called for silence.

"Oh, no!" Andro groaned. All the stars waited. Finally, Great Singing Star spoke.

"Andro Star, you are *not* singing in tune. I'm sorry, but you cannot sing with us when we sing our praises to the Lord God."

Andro could not hold back his tears. To think he still was not singing his part right! He had practiced *so* long. And he was trying *so* hard. The hot tears sparkled as they spilled down his sad face into the night sky.

"However," Great Singing Star continued, "you can be in your place right on the front row when we sing. And we want you to shine brightly. But don't make a sound! Not even one!"

Andro smiled a big thank you, and reached for a soft piece of cloud to wipe his tears. *All right then*, Andro thought, *I'll stand in my place and shine my very best!*

What a magnificent night it was! With sparkling faces the stars stood before the great white throne of the Lord God. And right in his place stood Andro, shining brightly with all his might.

On either side and behind the great white throne, angels stood quietly, reflecting the glow of the stars. This was the moment the star choir had waited for!

Bowing low before the Lord God, Great Singing Star spoke. "We have come to sing our songs of praise to You, Lord God of Heaven and Earth." Then raising his baton he led the star choir as their voices filled the heavens with glorious music.

Andro thought to himself, *Why this is the most wonderful moment of my life!* And his heart was so full of love for the Lord God he couldn't keep quiet. He began to hum, ever so softly. His gleaming face became a rainbow of light, glowing with all the beautiful colors you can imagine.

Andro thought he would burst with joy! He just had to sing. Just a little. Then, a little more and a little more. Louder and louder and LOUDER he sang with the stars.

When the song ended, and Great Singing Star had lowered his baton for silence, Andro was still singing. His loud voice rang out all over Heaven with praises to the Lord God—right from the bottom of his shining heart. And his song was not even the slightest, slightest, bit in tune.

"SHH! SHHH!!!" Andro heard the star next to him say out of the corner of his mouth.

When Andro realized what he had done, he felt terrible. He was soooo embarrassed that instantly his sparkling light turned a rosy red. Zooming off into the night sky, Andro turned his light out completely.

No matter where he went, he heard the comments of stars passing near him. "That Andro Star! Who does he think he is, anyway?"

"He ruined our songs of praise to the Lord God!" Andro heard them say. "He spoiled the whole thing!"

For a long, long time Andro did not shine, not even a little glow. He was too sad. No longer did he go zooming in and out among the other stars, leaving his silvery, sparkling trail of cosmic dust, the way he used to. He had not meant to spoil the songs of praise sung by the star choir. He only wanted the Lord God to know how much he loved Him, and how glad he was to be a shining star in the heavens.

God certainly must be disappointed in me, Andro thought over and over. *This was the worst mistake ever. How can I ever feel happy again?*

One night a dazzling, yellow shooting star skidded up to Andro.

"Hey, Andro," he said catching his breath, "have you seen what's goin' on? The angel of the Lord makin' all those flights to Earth?"

"I haven't noticed, I guess. What's it all mean?" Andro asked. But the shooting star was off and away before Andro even finished his question.

Soon Andro Star saw the Angel Gabriel zooming by on his way to Earth. There was a feeling of great excitement in the air. Something special was going to happen. The stars were whispering excitedly. Whatever could it all mean?

One night, soon after the moon had begun to shine upon Earth's eastern lands, the angel of the Lord came and stood by Andro. "Come with me," the angel commanded. "The Lord God wants to speak to you."

"ZipZappityZoom!" Andro said under his breath. "What have I done now?" He shook with fear. His light flickered as he followed closely behind the angel.

After what seemed to be a long, long time, the angel signaled him to stop. Andro heard the voice of the Lord God, like the sound of rushing waters. "Because of your loving heart, I have chosen you, Andro," the Lord God said, "for a most important mission. Go with my angel now. Do as he commands. I am expecting you to do your very best, Andro."

Traveling across the heavens, Andro was so excited and pleased he felt like singing. And he did, off tune, of course. Faster, faster, and faster he chased the angel past thousands and thousands of giant red stars, tiny white stars, sparkling blue stars, and meteroids crashing through space.

"Where are we going?" Andro called out when they slowed down to let a fiery comet whizz by. But the angel only said, "Wait and see!"

"ZipZappityZoom!" Andro gasped, seeing the most, the very *most* angels he had *ever* seen in one place. He turned to take another quick look. "ZipZappityZoom!"

Andro saw that they were approaching Earth. And now he was more curious than ever. The air was cold and crystal clear. On a hill just outside the little town of Bethlehem in Judea, a few shepherds huddled closely around a fire. Lambs nestled close to their mothers.

"Wait here," the angel commanded. "Shine only a soft light. Watch and listen. I will return."

All was quiet. Andro's eyes glowed with excitement. He watched the angel move closer and closer to Earth. Then, in an instant, the hillside became bright as day! Shining brightly with the glory of the Lord God, the angel came near the shepherds. They were terribly frightened.

"Don't be afraid," Andro heard the angel say. "I bring you the most joyful news ever told, and it's great news for everyone!" The shepherds were dazzled by the brightness, but they listened carefully.

"The Savior, yes, the Messiah, Son of the Lord God, has been born tonight in Bethlehem!"

So that's what all the excitement's been about in Heaven. Andro said to himself.

The angel spoke again to the shepherds, "How will you recognize Him? You will find a baby wrapped in swaddling clothes, lying in a manger."

When Andro heard this great news, he wanted to shine brightly and *show* how happy he was. "ZipZappityZoom," Andro said slowly under his breath. "God's Son! Born this night in Bethlehem!" But, before he became more excited, Andro remembered the angel's instructions. So only a soft light glowed from his joyful face.

Then suddenly before he could even say "ZipZappity-Zoom!" the BIGGEST choir of angels he had ever seen burst into song.

"Glory to God in the highest Heaven," they sang, "and peace on Earth to all who please Him."

Softly Andro began to sing. "OH! What a happy night this is!" He just *had* to sing to keep from bursting with joy! And when the angel choir finished their song, Andro was still singing. But ever so softly.

"Come on! Let's go to Bethlehem!" Andro heard one of the shepherds say. "Let's see this wonderful thing that has happened."

Andro smiled. "I wish I could show them the way. I could *really* light up those dark and narrow streets!" But he stayed right where the angel told him.

The shepherds ran down the hill to Bethlehem. They looked and looked until, just as the angel had said, they found the baby Jesus, lying in a manger. And close by was the baby's mother, Mary, and her husband, Joseph.

Andro was so busy watching the shepherds he was startled when the angel of the Lord touched his highest ray. "Stay here, Andro, and shine your *brightest* in this eastern sky," the angel instructed. And with that, he was gone.

Night after night, for many, many nights, Andro's brilliant light could be seen shining in the sky. People on Earth wondered and talked about this dazzling new star.

Then one evening when Andro was shining most brilliantly, a voice called to him. "Andro Star, Andro. Look over there!"

Andro looked where the angel was pointing. "You mean down there? Where those people are riding their camels out of Jerusalem?"

"That's right," the angel replied. "They are Wise-men from faraway lands. They have come to find the child Jesus. The Lord God has given *you* the special mission to show them where He is."

So, that's why I've been waiting here! Andro thought.

The angel continued. "These men have been watching you each evening as they traveled toward Jerusalem. And now *you* are to lead them with your light to the house where the child Jesus is." Then, just as quickly as he came, the angel was gone.

"Lead them with my light! Lead them with my light!" Andro smiled, repeating the angel's words. "Just think! The Lord God chose *me* to lead them to Jesus!!"

With much care, Andro aimed his rays just in front of the travelers as they rode on their camels toward Bethlehem. He noticed these men were dressed like kings. And they seemed to be in a great hurry.

Andro beamed his bright light along the narrow streets of Bethlehem. With his happy, strong rays, he led the Wise-men through the streets of Bethlehem—right to the house where Jesus lived with His family.

The Wise-men climbed off their camels. Their long, long journey was over. They looked up with grateful faces. Andro had shown them where to find the child Jesus.

The Wise-men entered the house, each one carrying something special in his hands. *It looks like they are bringing presents to Jesus*, Andro thought.

"Wish I had a present to give Him, too. I don't have anything to give. I—I can't even sing in tune for Him." Sadly, Andro's light began to dim.

And just at that moment, an angel's voice called, "Andro Star, I have a message for you. A message from the Lord God."

"A message for *me?*" Andro asked, amazed.

"Just for you, Andro." The angel spoke softly. "You completed your mission very well. Very well, indeed! You gave your light to guide the Wise-men to the child Jesus in Bethlehem."

"Well, I did do exactly as I was told," Andro replied.

"Your light was a very important gift of love and obedience to the Lord God," the angel continued. "Your gift will always be remembered in Heaven and on Earth."

The angel paused. Then, with a voice that could be heard all over the heavens, the angel announced: "No longer will you be called Andro Star. From this time on, your name is 'Star of Bethlehem'!"

"ZIPZAPPITYZOOM!!" That was all Andro could think to say.

Following the angel, Andro was surprised to see stars nodding and smiling at him all along the way.

As he neared highest Heaven, a voice called out, "Good morning, Star of Bethlehem!" It was the Great Singing Star himself.

And he did not even seem to notice that Andro was humming and singing—just a bit off tune.